For my wonderful
Grandson

Drayk Yanaba Johnson

with lots of love

Grandma Jann

2009.

NURSERY
TREASURY

Illustrated by
Jonathan Langley

BARNES
&NOBLE
BOOKS
NEW YORK

For Rachel, Katie, Natasha and Joseph

and Rosie

JL

CONTENTS

INTRODUCTION

When is a child ready to be introduced to the world of books— from the moment that child is born. All parents want to share favorite rhymes and songs from their childhood, but how do you recall those half-remembered fragments?

This collection brings together a treasure trove of timeless favorites from Nurseryland. The contents have been selected to fit every mood and situation and are designed to take the ever changing newborn on the road through infancy.

To begin with there are lullabies to help the baby sleep. Next come rhymes that encourage speech, and, as the baby starts to crawl and move freely, there are play rhymes to act out together. Later, as the toddler begins to speak fluently, there are funny songs and poems that develop a child's understanding of the world and feed the imagination. Finally, stories blend all the best ingredients of nursery writing and begin to bridge the gap between the safe world of the nursery and the bigger world of school and beyond.

To find all these things in one collection is unique. The *Collins Nursery Treasury* contains them all, enhanced by glorious pictures, to ensure that babies and toddlers get the very best start in life.

LULLABIES

Twinkle, twinkle, little star,
How I wonder what you are!
Up above the world so high,
Like a diamond in the sky.

When the blazing sun is gone,
When he nothing shines upon,
Then you show your little light,
Twinkle, twinkle, all the night.

Then the traveller in the dark,
Thanks you for your tiny spark;
He could not see which way to go,
If you did not twinkle so.

In the dark blue sky you keep,
And often through my curtains peep,
For you never shut your eye,
Till the sun is in the sky.

As your bright and tiny spark,
Lights the traveller in the dark,
Though I know not what you are,
Twinkle, twinkle, little star.

Jane Taylor

The Man in the Moon looked out of the moon,
Looked out of the moon and said,
"'Tis time for all children on the earth
To think about getting to bed!"

I see the moon,
And the moon sees me;
God bless the moon,
And God bless me.

Star light, star bright,
First star I see tonight,
   I wish I may,
   I wish I might,
Have the wish I wish tonight.

Hush, little baby, don't say a word,
Papa's gonna buy you a mockingbird.
If that mockingbird won't sing,
Papa's gonna buy you a diamond ring.

If that diamond ring turns brass,
Papa's gonna buy you a looking glass.
If that looking glass gets broke,
Papa's gonna buy you a billy goat.

If that billy goat won't pull,
Papa's gonna buy you a cart and bull.
If that cart and bull turn over,
Papa's gonna buy you a dog named Rover.

If that dog named Rover won't bark,
Papa's gonna buy you a horse and cart.
And if that horse and cart fall down,
You'll still be the sweetest little baby in town.

Bye, baby bunting,
Daddy's gone a-hunting,
To get a little rabbit's skin,
To wrap a baby bunting in.

Rock-a-bye, baby, on the tree top;
When the wind blows, the cradle will rock;
When the bough breaks, the cradle will fall,
Down will come baby, cradle and all.

Golden Slumbers kiss your eyes,
Smiles awake you when you rise:
Sleep, pretty darling, do not cry,
And I will sing a lullaby:
Lullaby, lullaby, lullaby.

Thomas Dekker

The sun descending in the west
The evening star does shine;
The birds are silent in their nest,
And I must seek for mine.
The moon like a flower
In heaven's high bower,
With silent delight
Sits and smiles on the night.

William Blake

Speed bonny boat like a bird on the wing,
Onward the sailor's cry.
Carry the lad that's born to be king
Over the sea to Skye.

Though the waves leap,
Soft shall you sleep,
Ocean's a royal bed.
Rock in the deep,
Flora will keep
Watch by your weary head.

Sweet and low, sweet and low,
  Wind of the western sea,
Low, low, breathe and blow,
  Wind of the western sea!
Over the rolling waters go,
  Come from the dying moon, and blow,
  Blow him again to me;
While my little one, while my pretty one sleeps.

  Father will come to his babe in the nest,
  Silver sails all out of the west
  Under the silver moon.
Sleep, my little one, sleep, my pretty one, sleep.

Lord Alfred Tennyson

Sleep, baby, sleep,
Your father keeps the sheep,
Your mother shakes a little tree,
A dream falls gently down for thee,
Sleep, baby, sleep.

Sleep, baby, sleep,
Your daddy keeps the sheep,
Your mother guards the lambs this night,
And keeps them safe till morning light,
Sleep, baby, sleep.

Sleep, baby, sleep,
In heaven lie the sheep,
The little lambs like stars of gold,
The moon's the shepherd of the fold,
Sleep, baby, sleep.

Teddy Bear, Teddy Bear,
  Go upstairs.
Teddy Bear, Teddy Bear,
  Say your prayers.
Teddy Bear, Teddy Bear,
  Turn out the light.
Teddy Bear, Teddy Bear,
  Say good night.

Now the day is over,
Night is drawing nigh,
Shadows of the evening
Steal across the sky.

Now the darkness gathers,
Stars begin to peep,
Birds and beasts and flowers
Soon will be asleep.

Sabine Baring-Gould

Sleepy time has come for my baby,
Baby now is going to sleep.
Kiss Mama goodnight
And we'll turn out the light,
While I tuck you in bed
'Neath your covers tight.
Sleepy time has come for my baby,
Baby now is going to sleep.

Little Boy Blue come blow your horn,
The sheep's in the meadow, the cow's in the corn.
Where is the boy who looks after the sheep?
He's under a haystack fast asleep.
Will you wake him? No, not I!
For if I do, he's sure to cry.

Sleep little child, go to sleep,
Mother is here by thy bed.
Sleep little child, go to sleep,
Rest on the pillow thy head.

The world is silent and still,
The moon shines bright on the hill,
Then creeps past the windowsill.

Sleep little child, go to sleep.
Oh sleep, go to sleep.

Lullaby, oh lullaby,
Flowers are closed and lambs are sleeping;
Stars are up, the moon is keeping,
Lullaby, oh lullaby.

While the birds are silence keeping,
Sleep my baby, fall a-sleeping,
Lullaby, oh lullaby,
Lullaby, oh lullaby.

Now good night.
Fold up your clothes
As you were taught,
Fold your two hands,
Fold up your thought;
Day is the plough-land,
Night is the stream,
Day is for doing
And night is for dream.
Now good night.

Eleanor Farjeon

Lullaby and good night,
With rosy bedlight,
With down over spread
Is baby's sweet bed.
Lay thee down now and rest,
May thy slumbers be blest,
Lay thee down now and rest,
May thy slumbers be blest.

Lullaby and goodnight,
Thy mother's delight.
Bright angels beside
My darling abide.
They will guard thee at rest,
Thou shall wake on my breast.
They will guard thee at rest,
Thou shall wake on my breast.

Johannes Brahms

The north wind doth blow,
And we shall have snow,
And what will the robin do then? Poor thing!
    He'll sit in a barn,
    And keep himself warm,
And hide his head under his wing. Poor thing!

The north wind doth blow,
And we shall have snow,
And what will the swallow do then? Poor thing!
    Oh, do you not know,
    That he's off long ago,
To a country where he will find spring. Poor thing!

The north wind doth blow,
And we shall have snow,
And what will the dormouse do then? Poor thing!
    Roll'd up like a ball,
    In his nest snug and small,
He'll sleep till warm weather comes in. Poor thing!

The north wind doth blow,
And we shall have snow,
And what will the honeybee do then? Poor thing!
    In his hive he will stay,
    Till the cold is away,
And then he'll come out in the spring. Poor thing!

The north wind doth blow,
And we shall snow,
And what will the children do then? Poor things!
    When lessons are done,
    They must skip, jump and run,
Until they have made themselves warm. Poor things!

Sweet babe, a golden cradle holds thee,
Sewn of snow, a fleece enfolds thee,
Fairest flowers are strewn before thee,
 Sweet birds warble o'er thee.

Oh sleep, my baby free from sorrow,
Bright then look thine eyes tomorrow,
Sleep while all thy smiling slumbers,
 Angels all chant their numbers.

Moon, sun, shiny and silver,
Moon, sun, shiny and gold,
Moon, sun, shine on the young ones,
Shine until they grow old.

Shine, shine, shine, shine,
Shine until they grow old.

Far in the wood, you'll find a well,
With water deep and blue,
Whoever drinks by moonlight clear
Will live a thousand years.

And all around the little well
Are seven lovely trees.
They rock and sway and sing a song,
My baby, all for you.

The dark is dreaming,
    Day is done,
Good night, good night
    To everyone.

Good night to the birds,
    And the fish in the sea,
Good night to the bears,
    And good night to me.

Dennis Lee

The soft shades are creeping,
My heart's love the angels are near.
Hush, oh, my treasure is dreaming,
    Oh, sleep on till day.

My darling is sleeping
While mother is near,
Smiles now are beaming,
    Sorrows away.

In your white cradle lying,
God give you
Your night's sweet repose.
Hush, oh, my treasure is dreaming,
    Oh, sleep on till day.

Sleep sweet babe, my care beguiling,
Mother beside thee is smiling.
If thou sleep not, mother doth mourn,
Singing as the wheel she turns,
Sleep, darling, tenderly,
Come, slumber, balmily.

Nursery Rhymes

There was an old woman who lived in a shoe.
She had so many children she didn't know what to do.
She gave them some broth without any bread.
She told them off soundly and sent them to bed.

There was a crooked man, and he walked a crooked mile,
He found a crooked sixpence against a crooked stile;
He bought a crooked cat, which caught a crooked mouse,
And they all lived together in a little crooked house.

Higglety, pigglety, pop!
The dog has eaten the mop;
  The pig's in a hurry,
  The cat's in a flurry,
Higglety, pigglety, pop!

Humpty Dumpty sat on a wall,
Humpty Dumpty had a great fall.
   All the king's horses
   And all the king's men
Couldn't put Humpty together again.

Old King Cole
Was a merry old soul,
And a merry old soul was he;
He called for his pipe,
And he called for his bowl,
And he called for his fiddlers three.

Every fiddler he had a fiddle,
And a very fine fiddle had he;
Oh, there's none so rare
As can compare
With King Cole and his fiddlers three.

Oh, the grand old Duke of York,
He had ten thousand men;
He marched them up
To the top of the hill,
And he marched them down again.

And when they were up, they were up,
And when they were down, they were down,
And when they were only halfway up,
They were neither up nor down.

Hey diddle, diddle,
The cat and the fiddle,
The cow jumped over the moon;
The little dog laughed
To see such sport,
And the dish ran away with the spoon.

Ride a cockhorse to Banbury Cross,
To see a fine lady upon a white horse;
Rings on her fingers and bells on her toes,
She shall have music wherever she goes.

Wee Willie Winkie runs through the town,
Upstairs and downstairs in his nightgown,
Tapping at the windows, crying through the locks,
"Are all the children in their beds, it's now eight o'clock?"

Girls and boys, come out to play,
The moon doth shine as bright as day;
Leave your supper and leave your sleep,
And join your playfellows in the street.
Come with a whoop and come with a call,
Come with a goodwill or not at all.
Up the ladder and down the wall,
A halfpenny roll will serve us all.
You find milk, and I'll find flour,
And we'll have a pudding in half an hour.

Georgy Porgy, pudding and pie,
Kissed the girls and made them cry.
When the boys came out to play,
Georgy Porgy ran away.

Jack and Jill
Went up the hill,
To fetch a pail of water;
Jack fell down,
And broke his crown,
And Jill came tumbling after.

Then up Jack got,
And home did trot,
As fast as he could caper;
He went to bed,
To mend his head,
With vinegar and brown paper.

Baa, baa, black sheep,
Have you any wool?
Yes, sir, yes, sir,
Three bags full;
One for the master,
And one for the dame,
And one for the little boy
Who lives down the lane.

Mary had a little lamb,
Its fleece was white as snow;
And everywhere that Mary went
The lamb was sure to go.

It followed her to school one day,
Which was against the rule;
It made the children laugh and play,
To see a lamb at school.

And so the teacher turned it out,
But still it lingered near,
And waited patiently about
Till Mary did appear.

"Why does the lamb love Mary so?"
The eager children cry.
"Why, Mary loves the lamb, you know,"
The teacher did reply.

Old Mother Hubbard
Went to the cupboard,
To fetch her poor dog a bone.
When she got there,
The cupboard was bare,
And so the poor dog had none.

Little Miss Muffet
Sat on a tuffet,
Eating her curds and whey;
Along came a spider,
Who sat down beside her
And frightened Miss Muffet away.

Hickory, dickory, dock,
The mouse ran up the clock.
The clock struck one,
The mouse ran down,
Hickory, dickory, dock.

The Queen of Hearts,
She made some tarts,
All on a summer's day.
The Knave of Hearts,
He stole the tarts,
And took them clean away.

The King of Hearts
Called for the tarts,
And beat the Knave full sore.
The Knave of Hearts
Brought back the tarts
And vowed he'd steal no more.

Little Jack Horner
Sat in the corner,
Eating a Christmas pie;
He put in his thumb,
And pulled out a plum,
And said, "What a good boy am I!"

One, two,
Buckle my shoe;
Three, four,
Knock at the door;
Five, six,
Pick up sticks;
Seven, eight,
Lay them straight;
Nine, ten,
A big fat hen;
Eleven, twelve,
Dig and delve;
Thirteen, fourteen,
Maids a-courting;
Fifteen, sixteen,
Maids in the kitchen;
Seventeen, eighteen,
Maids in waiting;
Nineteen, twenty,
My plate's empty.

PLAY RHYMES

IF YOU'RE HAPPY AND YOU KNOW IT

If you're happy and you know it, clap your hands.
If you're happy and you know it, clap your hands.
If you're happy and you know it and you really want to show it,
If you're happy and you know it, clap your hands.

If you're happy and you know it, nod your head.
If you're happy and you know it, nod your head.
If you're happy and you know it and you really want to show it,
If you're happy and you know it, nod your head.

If you're happy and you know it, stamp your feet.
If you're happy and you know it, stamp your feet.
If you're happy and you know it and you really want to show it,
If you're happy and you know it, stamp your feet.

If you're happy and you know it, say "we are."
If you're happy and you know it, say "we are."
If you're happy and you know it and you really want to show it,
If you're happy and you know it, say "we are."

If you're happy and you know it, do all four.
If you're happy and you know it, do all four.
If you're happy and you know it and you really want to show it,
If you're happy and you know it, do all four.

This is the way the ladies ride,
  Nim, nim, nim, nim.
This is the way the gentlemen ride,
  Trim, trim, trim, trim.
This is the way the farmers ride,
  Trot, trot, trot, trot.
This is the way the huntsmen ride,
  A-gallop, a-gallop, a-gallop.
This is the way the ploughboys ride,
  Hobble-de-hoy, hobble-de-hoy.

This little piggy went to market;
This little piggy stayed home;
This little piggy had roast beef;
This little piggy had none;
And this little piggy cried, "Wee! Wee! Wee!"
  All the way home.

A farmer went trotting upon his grey mare,
　Bumpety, bumpety bump!
With his daughter behind him so rosy and fair,
　Lumpety, lumpety, lump!

A magpie cried "Caw," and they all tumbled down,
　Bumpety, bumpety, bump!
The mare broke her knees, and the farmer his crown,
　Lumpety, lumpety, lump!

The mischievous magpie flew laughing away,
　Bumpety, bumpety, bump!
And vowed he would serve them the same the next day,
　Lumpety, lumpety, lump!

Round and round the garden,
Goes the Teddy Bear,
　One step,
　Two step,
Tickle you under there!

Two little dicky-birds
Sitting on a wall,
One named Peter, one named Paul.
Fly away Peter, fly away Paul;
Come back Peter,
Come back Paul.

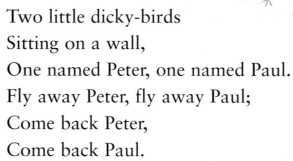

Two little blackbirds singing in the sun,
One flew away and then there was one.
One little blackbird, very black and small,
He flew away and then there was the wall.
One little brick wall lonely in the rain,
Waiting for the blackbirds to come and sing again.

Five little ducks went swimming one day,
Over the hills and far away.
Mother Duck said, "Quack, quack, quack, quack."
But only four little ducks came back.

Four little ducks went swimming one day,
Over the hills and far away.
Mother Duck said, "Quack, quack, quack, quack."
But only three little ducks came back.

Three little ducks went swimming one day,
Over the hills and far away.
Mother Duck said, "Quack, quack, quack, quack."
But only two little ducks came back.

Two little ducks went swimming one day,
Over the hills and far away.
Mother Duck said, "Quack, quack, quack, quack."
But only one little duck came back.

One little duck went swimming one day,
Over the hills and far away.
Mother Duck said, "Quack, quack, quack, quack."

But no little ducks came back.

Five currant buns in a baker's shop,
Round and fat with sugar on the top.
Along came a boy with a penny one day,
Bought a currant bun and took it away.

Two little eyes to look around,
Two little ears to hear each sound,
One little nose to smell what's sweet,
One little mouth that likes to eat.

I'm a little teapot, short and stout;
Here is my handle, here is my spout.
When I start to whistle, hear me shout,
"Tip me over and pour me out."

Down by the station, early in the morning,
See the little puffer trains all in a row.
See the engine driver pull the little handle.
Choo, choo, choo, and off we go.

Down at the farmyard early in the morning,
See the little tractor standing in the barn.
Do you see the farmer pull the little handle?
Chug, chug, chug, and off we go.

Here is a steamroller, rolling and rolling,
Ever so slowly, because of its load.
Then it rolls up to the top of the hill,
Puffing and panting it has to stand still.
Then it rolls... all the way down!

THE HOKEY POKEY

You put your right arm in, you take your right arm out,
You put your right arm in, and you shake it all about.
You do the hokey pokey
And you turn yourself around,
That's what it's all about.

You put your left arm in, you take your left arm out,
You put your left arm in, and you shake it all about.
You do the hokey pokey
And you turn yourself around,
That's what it's all about.

You put your right leg in, you take your right leg out,
You put your right leg in, and you shake it all about.
You do the hokey pokey
And you turn yourself around,
That's what it's all about.

You put your left leg in, you take your left leg out,
You put your left leg in, and you shake it all about.
You do the hokey pokey
And you turn yourself around,
That's what it's all about.

You put your head in, you take your head out,
You put your head in, and you shake it all about.
You do the hokey pokey
And you turn yourself around,
That's what it's all about.

You put your whole self in, you take your whole self out,
You put your whole self in, and you shake yourself about.
You do the hokey pokey
And you turn yourself around,
That's what it's all about.

Here is the church,
Here is the steeple,
Open the doors
And here are the people.
Here's the parson going upstairs,
And here he is a-saying his prayers.

Head and shoulders, knees and toes,
Knees and toes, knees and toes,
Head and shoulders, knees and toes,
We all turn round together.

Incy Wincy Spider climbed up the water spout,
Down came the rain drops and washed poor incy out;
Out came the sunshine and dried up all the rain,
And Incy Wincy spider climbed up the spout again.

SONGS

Lavender's blue, dilly, dilly,
Lavender's green.
When I am king, dilly, dilly,
You shall be queen.
Who told you so, dilly, dilly,
Who told you so?
'Twas mine own heart, dilly, dilly,
That told me so.

Call up your men, dilly, dilly,
Set them to work;
Some with a rake, dilly, dilly,
Some with a fork;
Some to make hay, dilly, dilly,
Some to thresh corn;
Whilst you and I, dilly, dilly,
Keep ourselves warm.

One, two, three, four, five,
Once I caught a fish alive;
Six, seven, eight, nine, ten,
Then I let him go again.
Why did you let him go?
Because he bit my finger so.
Which finger did he bite?
This little finger on my right.

Little Bo-Peep has lost her sheep,
And doesn't know where to find them.
Leave them alone, and they'll come home
Bringing their tails behind them.

Little Bo-Peep fell fast asleep,
And dreamt she heard them bleating.
But when she awoke, she found it a joke,
For they were still a-fleeting.

Then up she took her little crook
Determined for to find them;
She found them indeed, but it made her heart bleed,
For they'd left all their tails behind them.

It happened one day, as Bo-Peep did stray
Into a meadow hard by.
There she espied their tails side by side,
All hung on a tree to dry.

She heaved a sigh, and wiped her eye
And over the hillocks went rambling,
And tried what she could,
    as a shepherdess should,
To tack again each to its lambkin.

THE WHEELS ON THE BUS

The wheels on the bus go round and round, round and round, round and round,
The wheels on the bus go round and round, all through the town.

The people on the bus go up and down, up and down, up and down,
The people on the bus go up and down, all through the town.

The driver on the bus yells "Move on back," "Move on back," "Move on back",
The driver on the bus yells "Move on back," all through the town.

The horn on the bus goes beep, beep, beep; beep, beep, beep; beep, beep, beep,
The horn on the bus goes beep, beep, beep, all through the town.

The wipers on the bus go swish, swish, swish; swish, swish, swish; swish,
    swish, swish,
The wipers on the bus go swish, swish, swish, all through the town.

The babies on the bus go waagh, waagh, waagh; waagh, waagh, waagh; waagh,
    waagh, waagh,
The babies on the bus go waagh, waagh, waagh, all through the town.

OLD McDONALD

Old McDonald had a farm,
  E...I...E...I...O
And on that farm he had some cows,
  E...I...E...I...O
With a moo-moo here,
And a moo-moo there,
  Here a moo,
  There a moo,
Everywhere a moo-moo,
Old McDonald had a farm,
  E...I...E...I...O.

Old McDonald had a farm,
  E...I...E...I...O
And on that farm he had some ducks,
  E...I...E...I...O
With a quack-quack here,
And a quack-quack there,
  Here a quack,
  There a quack,
Everywhere a quack-quack;
With a moo-moo here,
And a moo-moo there,
  Here a moo,
  There a moo,
Everywhere a moo-moo,
Old McDonald had a farm,
  E...I...E...I...O.

Old McDonald had a farm,
E...I...E...I...O
And on that farm he had some sheep,
E...I...E...I...O
With a baa-baa here,
And a baa-baa there,
Here a baa,
There a baa,
Everywhere a baa-baa,
With a quack-quack here,
And a quack-quack there,
Here a quack,
There a quack,
Everywhere a quack-quack;
With a moo-moo here,
And a moo-moo there,
Here a moo,
There a moo,
Everywhere a moo-moo,
Old McDonald had a farm,
E...I...E...I...O.

Old McDonald had a farm,
E...I...E...I...O
And on that farm he had some pigs,
E...I...E...I...O
With an oink-oink here,
And an oink-oink there,
Here an oink,
There an oink,
Everywhere an oink-oink;
With a baa-baa here,
And a baa-baa there,
Here a baa,
There a baa,
Everywhere a baa-baa,
With a quack-quack here,
And a quack-quack there,
Here a quack,
There a quack,
Everywhere a quack-quack;
With a moo-moo here,
And a moo-moo there,
Here a moo,
There a moo,
Everywhere a moo-moo,
Old McDonald had a farm,
E...I...E...I...O.

Ring around the roses,
A pocket full of posies,
   Ashes, ashes,
We all fall down.

The king has sent his daughter
To fetch a pail of water,
   Ashes, ashes,
We all fall down.

The robin on the steeple
Is singing to the people,
   Ashes, ashes,
We all fall down.

Pat-a-cake, pat-a-cake, baker's man,
Bake me a cake as fast as you can!
Pat it and prick it and mark it with 'B'
And put it in the oven for baby and me.

Oh, dear, what can the matter be?
Dear, dear, what can the matter be?
Oh, dear, what can the matter be?
Johnny's so long at the fair.

He promised to buy me a pair of sleeve buttons,
A pair of new garters that cost him but two cents,
He promised he'd bring me a bunch of blue ribbons
To tie up my bonny brown hair.

And it's oh, dear, what can the matter be?
Dear, dear, what can the matter be?
Oh, dear, what can the matter be?
Johnny's so long at the fair.

He promised he'd buy me a basket of roses,
A garland of lilies, a garland of posies,
A little straw hat to set off the blue ribbons,
That tie up my bonny brown hair.

Oh, dear, what can the matter be?
Dear, dear, what can the matter be?
Oh, dear, what can the matter be?
Johnny's so long at the fair.

The big ship sails on the alley-alley-o, the alley-alley-o, the alley-alley-o,
The big ship sails on the alley-alley-o, on the last day of September.

The captain said it will never, never do, never, never do, never, never do,
The captain said it will never, never do, on the last day of September.

The big ship sank to the bottom of the sea, the bottom of the sea,
   the bottom of the sea,
The big ship sank to the bottom of the sea, on the last day of September.

We all dip our heads in the deep blue sea, the deep blue sea,
   the deep blue sea,
We all dip our heads in the deep blue sea, on the last day of September.

Row, row, row your boat,
Gently down the stream.
Merrily, merrily, merrily, merrily,
Life is but a dream.

DONKEY RIDING

Were you ever in Quebec,
Stowing timbers on a deck,
Where there's a king in his golden crown
    Riding on a donkey?

Hey ho, and away we go,
Donkey riding, donkey riding,
Hey ho, and away we go,
    Riding on a donkey.

Were you ever in Cardiff Bay,
Where the folks all shout, "Hooray!
Here comes John with his three months' pay,
    Riding on a donkey?"

Hey ho, and away we go,
Donkey riding, donkey riding,
Hey ho, and away we go,
    Riding on a donkey.

Were you ever off Cape Horn,
Where it's always fine and warm?
See the lion and the unicorn
    Riding on a donkey.

Hey ho, and away we go,
Donkey riding, donkey riding,
Hey ho, and away we go,
    Riding on a donkey.

ONE MAN WENT TO MOW

One man went to mow, went to mow a meadow,
One man and his dog went to mow a meadow.

Two men went to mow, went to mow a meadow,
Two men, one man and his dog went to mow a meadow.

Three men went to mow, went to mow a meadow,
Three men, two men, one man and his dog went to mow a meadow.

Four men went to mow, went to mow a meadow,
Four men, three men, two men, one man and his dog went to mow
   a meadow.

Five men went to mow, went to mow a meadow,
Five men, four men, three men, two men, one man and his dog went
   to mow a meadow.

Six men went to mow, went to mow a meadow,
Six men, five men, four men, three men, two men, one man and his dog
   went to mow a meadow.

Seven men went to mow, went to mow a meadow,
Seven men, six men, five men, four men, three men, two men, one man
 and his dog went to mow a meadow.

Eight men went to mow, went to mow a meadow,
Eight men, seven men, six men, five men, four men, three men, two men,
 one man and his dog went to mow a meadow.

Nine men went to mow, went to mow a meadow,
Nine men, eight men, seven men, six men, five men, four men, three men,
 two men, one man and his dog went to mow a meadow.

Ten men went to mow, went to mow a meadow,
Ten men, nine men, eight men, seven men, six men, five men, four men,
 three men, two men, one man and his dog went to mow a meadow.

ORANGES AND LEMONS

"Oranges and lemons," say the bells of St Clement's.
"You owe me five farthings," say the bells of St Martin's.
"When will you pay me?" say the bells of Old Bailey.
"When I grow rich," say the bells of Shoreditch.
"Pray when will that be?" say the bells of Stepney.
"I'm sure I don't know," says the great bell of Bow.

Here comes the candle to light you to bed,
And here comes a chopper to chop off your head.
Chip chop, chip chop,
The last man's head.

POP GOES THE WEASEL

Half a pound of two penny rice,
Half a pound of treacle,
That's the way the money goes,
Pop goes the weasel!

Up and down the city road,
In and out the eagle,
That's the way the money goes,
Pop goes the weasel!

Every night when I go out,
The monkey's on the table,
Take a stick and knock it off,
Pop goes the weasel!

A penny for a ball of thread,
Another for a needle,
That's the way the money goes,
Pop goes the weasel!

All around the cobbler's bench,
The monkey chased the weasel;
The donkey thought 'twas all in fun,
Pop goes the weasel!

THIS OLD MAN

This old man, he played one,
He played knick knack on my drum;
With a knick knack paddy whack, give a dog a bone,
   This old man came rolling home.

This old man, he played two,
He played knick knack on my shoe;
With a knick knack paddy whack, give a dog a bone,
   This old man came rolling home.

This old man, he played three,
He played knick knack on my tree;
With a knick knack paddy whack, give a dog a bone,
   This old man came rolling home.

This old man, he played four,
He played knick knack on my door;
With a knick knack paddy whack, give a dog a bone,
   This old man came rolling home.

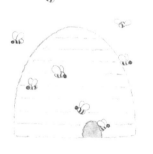

This old man, he played five,
He played knick knack on my hive
With a knick knack paddy whack, give a dog a bone,
   This old man came rolling home.

This old man, he played six,
He played knick knack on my sticks;
With a knick knack paddy whack, give a dog a bone,
This old man came rolling home.

This old man, he played seven,
He played knick knack down in Devon;
With a knick knack paddy whack, give a dog a bone,
This old man came rolling home.

This old man, he played eight,
He played knick knack on my gate;
With a knick knack paddy whack, give a dog a bone,
This old man came rolling home.

This old man, he played nine,
He played knick knack on my line;
With a knick knack paddy whack, give a dog a bone,
This old man came rolling home.

This old man, he played ten,
He played knick knack on my hen;
With a knick knack paddy whack, give a dog a bone,
This old man came rolling home.

Sing a song of sixpence,
A pocket full of rye;
Four-and-twenty blackbirds
Baked in a pie!

When the pie was opened,
The birds began to sing;
Wasn't that a dainty dish
To set before the king?

The king was in his counting-house,
Counting out his money;
The queen was in the parlor,
Eating bread and honey.

The maid was in the garden,
Hanging out the clothes,
When down came a blackbird
And pecked off her nose.

POEMS

THE MITTEN SONG

"Thumbs in the thumb-place,
Fingers all together!"
This is the song
We sing in mitten-weather.
When it is cold,
It doesn't matter whether
Mittens are wool,
Or made of finest leather.
This is the song
We sing in mitten-weather:
"Thumbs in the thumb-place,
Fingers all together!"

Marie Louise Allen

A sailor went to sea, sea, sea
To see what he could see, see, see.
But all that he could see, see, see,
Was the bottom of the deep blue sea, sea, sea!

64

It's raining, it's pouring,
The old man is snoring;
He went to bed and bumped his head
And couldn't get up in the morning!

HAPPINESS

John had
Great Big
Waterproof
Boots on;
John had a
Great Big
Waterproof
Hat;

John had a
Great Big
Waterproof
Mackintosh –
And that
(Said John)
Is
That.

A. A. Milne

PATCHY BEAR

I'm a roly-poly
plump teddy bear,
with a lopsided smile
and gold-coloured fur.

I've lost my growl
and a lot of my hair,
I'm old and I'm bald
and my fur has gone bare.

but I love to be cuddled
and snuggle in bed,
I need someone to say
You're my very best Ted.

I like listening to stories
to dance and to play,
I can keep secrets
and I'll do what you say.

I need someone special
a friend just like you,
so take care of me
and I'll take care of you.

Joan Poulson

MY TEDDY BEAR

A teddy bear is nice to hold.
The one I have is getting old.
His paws are almost wearing out
And so's his funny furry snout
From rubbing on my nose of skin,
And all his fur is pretty thin.
A ribbon and a piece of string
Make a sort of necktie thing.
His eyes came out and now instead
He has some new ones made of thread.
I take him everywhere I go
And tell him all the things I know.
I like the way he feels at night,
All snuggled up against me tight.

Margaret Hillert

Fuzzy Wuzzy was a bear,
Fuzzy Wuzzy had no hair.
Fuzzy Wuzzy wasn't fuzzy,
Was he?

LITTLE PICTURES

Little pictures
Hang above me.
Pictures of the folks
Who love me.
Mom and Dad
and Uncle Jack,
They love me...
I love them back.

Arnold Lobel

UP TO THE CEILING

Daddy lifts me
up to the ceiling.
Daddy swings me
down to the floor.
Daddy! Daddy!
More! More! MORE!
Up to the ceiling,
down to the floor.

Charles Thomson

There was a little girl, who had a little curl
Right in the middle of her forehead.
When she was good, she was very, very good,
But when she was bad, she was horrid.

Henry Wadsworth Longfellow

Cocks crow in the morn
To tell us to rise,
And he who lies late
Will never be wise;
For early to bed
And early to rise,
Is the way to be healthy
And wealthy and wise.

Monday's child is fair of face,
Tuesday's child is full of grace,
Wednesday's child is full of woe,
Thursday's child has far to go,
Friday's child is loving and giving,
Saturday's child works hard for a living;
And a child that is born on the Sabbath day
Is fair, and wise, and good, and gay.

One for sorrow, two for joy,
Three for a girl, four for a boy,
Five for silver, six for gold,
Seven for a secret ne'er to be told.

How many days has my baby to play?
Saturday, Sunday, Monday,
Tuesday, Wednesday, Thursday, Friday,
Saturday, Sunday, Monday.
Hop away, skip away,
My baby wants to play.
My baby wants to play every day.

BABY'S DRINKING SONG

Sip a little
Sup a little
  From your little
Cup a little
  Sup a little
Sip a little
  Put it to your
Lip a little
  Tip a little
Tap a little
  Not into your
Lap or it'll
  Drip a little
Drop a little
  On the table
Top a little.

James Kirkup

INFANT JOY

"I have no name,
I am but two days old."
What shall I call thee?
"I happy am,
Joy is my name."
Sweet joy befall thee!

Pretty Joy!
Sweet Joy, but two days old,
Sweet Joy I call thee;
Thou dost smile,
I sing the while;
Sweet joy befall thee!

William Blake

THE OWL AND THE PUSSYCAT

The Owl and the Pussycat went to sea
   In a beautiful pea-green boat,
They took some honey, and plenty of money,
   Wrapped up in a five-pound note.
The Owl looked up to the stars above,
   And sang to a small guitar,
"O lovely Pussy! O Pussy, my love,
   "What a beautiful Pussy you are,
     "You are,
     "You are!
   "What a beautiful Pussy you are!"

Pussy said to the Owl, "You elegant fowl!
   How charmingly sweet you sing!
"O let us be married; too long we have tarried:
   But what shall we do for a ring?"
They sailed away for a year and a day,
   To the land where the bong-tree grows,
And there in a wood a Piggy-wig stood,
   With a ring at the end of his nose,
     His nose,
     His nose,
   With a ring at the end of his nose.

"Dear Pig, are you willing to sell for one shilling
     Your ring?" Said the Piggy, "I will."
So they took it away, and were married next day
     By the Turkey who lives on the hill.
They dined on mince, and slices of quince,
     Which they ate with a runcible spoon;
And hand in hand, on the edge of the sand,
     They danced by the light of the moon,
          The moon,
          The moon,
     They danced by the light of the moon.

Edward Lear

If you should meet a Crocodile
Don't take a stick and poke him;
Ignore the welcome in his smile,
Be careful not to stroke him.
For as he sleeps upon the Nile,
He thinner gets and thinner;
And whene'er you meet a Crocodile
He's ready for his dinner.

Tinker, tailor,
Soldier, sailor,
Rich man, poor man,
Beggar man, thief.

STORIES

HENNY-PENNY

One day Henny-Penny was pecking at corn in the farmyard when an acorn fell on her head.

"Goodness me," clucked Henny-Penny. "The sky is falling. I must go and tell the king." She left quickly to find the king. On the way she met Cocky-Locky.

"Where are you going so fast?" crowed Cocky-Locky.

"The sky is falling," said Henny-Penny, "and I'm going to tell the king."

"Then I will come with you," said Cocky-Locky, and off he strutted with Henny-Penny. On the way they met Ducky-Lucky.

"Where are you two going so fast?" quacked Ducky-Lucky.

"The sky is falling," said Henny-Penny, "and we're going to tell the king."

"Then I will come with you," said Ducky-Lucky and off she waddled with Cocky-Locky and Henny-Penny. On the way they met Goosey-Loosey.

"Where are you three going so fast?" cackled Goosey-Loosey.

"The sky is falling," said Henny-Penny, "and we're going to tell the king."

"Then I will come with you," said Goosey-Loosey, and off he swaggered with Ducky-Lucky, Cocky-Locky and Henny-Penny.

On the way they met Foxy-Loxy.

"Where are you four going so fast?" asked Foxy-Loxy.

"The sky is falling," said Henny-Penny, "and we're going to tell the king."

"But you're going the wrong way," said Foxy-Loxy. "Follow me and I'll take you to the king."

So Goosey-Loosey, Ducky-Lucky, Cocky-Locky and Henny-Penny all followed Foxy-Loxy until they came to a dark cave.

"Follow me," said Foxy-Loxy, as she entered the cave, "this is the quickest way to the king." The cave was really the home of Foxy-Loxy, and she smiled to herself as the others followed her in.

Goosey-Loosey entered the cave first, followed by, Ducky-Lucky, and Cocky-Locky.

Henny-Penny was just about to follow when she heard Cocky-Locky screech, "COCK-A-DOODLE-DOO." Henny-Penny turned and ran as fast as she could back to the farmyard while Foxy-Loxy enjoyed a delicious dinner of Goosey-Loosey, Ducky-Lucky and Cocky-Locky.

So Henny-Penny never did tell the king the sky was falling and, in fact, the sky never did fall.

THE THREE LITTLE PIGS

Once upon a time there were three little pigs. One day their mother announced that the time had come for them to leave home and seek their fortunes. She packed their bags and waved them goodbye.

When they came to the crossroads they said farewell, and each of the three little pigs took a different road.

The first pig met a man with a bundle of straw and said to him, "Please, man, give me your straw to build a house." The man gave him the straw and he built his house with it. Soon along came a wolf who knocked on the door and said, "Little pig, little pig, let me come in."

"Not by the hair of my chinny-chin-chin," replied the little pig.

"Then I'll huff and I'll puff and I'll blow your house in," said the wolf. So he huffed and he puffed and he blew the house in and ate up the little pig.

The second pig met a man with a bundle of sticks and said, "Please, man, give me your sticks to build a house." The man gave him the sticks and he built his house with them. Soon the wolf came knocking at the door, "Little pig, little pig, let me come in."

"Not by the hair of my chinny-chin-chin," said the little pig.

"Then I'll huff and I'll puff and I'll blow your house in." And he huffed and he puffed and he blew the house in and ate up the little pig.

The third pig met a man with a load of bricks and said, "Please, man, give me your bricks to build a house." The man gave him the bricks and he built his house with them. Once again the wolf came and said, "Little pig, little pig, let me come in."

"Not by the hair of my chinny-chin-chin," said the little pig.

"Then I'll huff and I'll puff and I'll blow your house in." And he huffed and he puffed and he puffed and he huffed but he could not blow the house in.

The wolf was so angry that he jumped up on the roof and roared, "Little pig, little pig, I'll climb down your chimney and eat you up."

Quickly the little pig hung a pot of water over the fire. When the wolf came down the chimney he fell - SPLASH - into the boiling water. That was the end of the wolf and the clever little pig lived happily ever after.

THE GINGERBREAD BOY

Once upon a time there was a little old man and a little old woman. They hadn't any children of their own so one day the old woman decided to bake a gingerbread boy. She mixed up the dough, rolled it out and cut out the shape of a little boy with a big smile and two shiny, black currants for eyes. Then she popped it in the oven to bake.

When the gingerbread smelled good and ready, the little old woman opened the door of the oven. Much to her surprise, the gingerbread boy jumped out and ran away through the kitchen door calling,

"Run, run as fast as you can,

You can't catch me,

I'm the gingerbread man."

The old woman called her husband and they both chased after the gingerbread boy. But he was too fast for them and he jumped over the garden wall and into a farm.

"Oink, oink," called a pig, "won't you stop little gingerbread boy! I'd like to gobble you up." But the gingerbread boy just laughed.

"I've run away from a little old man and a little old woman, and I'll run away from you too."

The pig was too fat to catch the gingerbread boy who ran on and on until he came to a horse.

"Neigh, neigh," called the horse, "won't you stop little gingerbread boy. I'd like to gobble you up."

"I've run away from a little old man and a little old woman and a pig," laughed the gingerbread boy, "and I'll run away from you too."

"Run, run, as fast as you can,

You can't catch me,

I'm the gingerbread man."

The horse could gallop very quickly, so the gingerbread boy had to run as fast as his little gingerbread legs would carry him. But he escaped from the horse too, and was feeling very pleased with himself – until he came to a river that was deep and wide. A clever fox saw the gingerbread boy standing by the river and came to offer his help.

"If you ride on my back, I will carry you across the river," said the fox.

"Thank you," said the gingerbread boy and he jumped on to the fox's back.

They were halfway across the river when the fox said, "Jump on to my head, little gingerbread boy, then you won't get wet."

"Thank you," said the gingerbread boy and he jumped on to the fox's head.

The fox swam on further and then said, "Jump on to my nose, little gingerbread boy, then you won't get wet."

"Thank you," said the gingerbread boy and he jumped on to the fox's nose.

No sooner had he done so, than the fox threw back his head, opened his big mouth and SNIP-SNAP, he gobbled up the gingerbread boy. And that was the end of the little gingerbread boy.

GOLDILOCKS AND THE THREE BEARS

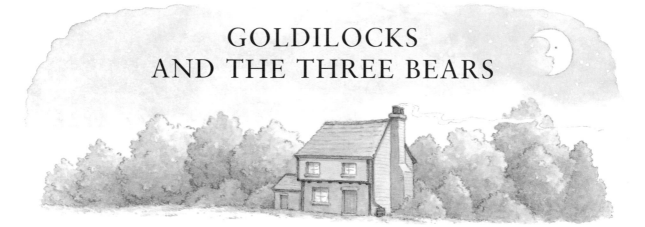

Once upon a time there was a family of three bears, Father Bear, Mother Bear and Baby Bear.

The Three Bears lived very happily together in a little house in a big wood. They each had their own special things. They had their own bowls: a big one for Father Bear, a middle-sized one for Mother Bear and a little one with rabbits on it for Baby Bear. They had their own chairs: a big one with a high back and arms for Father Bear; a middle-sized one with soft cushions for Mother Bear and a little one with rabbits on it for Baby Bear. They had their own beds: a big one for Father Bear; a middle-sized one for Mother Bear and a little one with rabbits on it for Baby Bear.

One morning Father Bear made a big pot of porridge for breakfast and poured it into the three bowls. It was still too hot to eat so Father Bear suggested that they all go for a stroll in the woods while the porridge cooled.

On that same morning a little girl called Goldilocks was walking in the woods. When she came to The Threc Bears' house and smelled the warm, delicious smell of porridge, she began to feel very hungry. She knocked on the door and, when there was no reply, she stepped inside and saw the three bowls of porridge on the table. First she tried the biggest bowl with the most amount of porridge in it.

"Oooh!" said Goldilocks. "Too hot."

Next she tried the middle-sized bowl.

"Yuk, too cold!" she said.

Then she tried the little bowl with the rabbits .

"Yum, yum just right," she said, and quickly ate it all up.

Goldilocks started to make herself at home. She tried sitting in the biggest chair but it was very uncomfortable.

"Too hard," said Goldilocks.

Then she tried the middle-sized chair.

"Aaarrggh!" she cried as she sank right into the cushions. "Too soft."

Next she tried the little chair.

"Mmm, just right," she said. She liked this one and wriggled with glee, so much so that - CRASH! - the chair broke and she fell to the floor.

Picking herself up, Goldilocks decided to explore the upstairs, where she found the three beds. First she tried lying on the biggest bed.

"Too high," she said.

Next she tried lying on the middle-sized bed.

"Too low," said Goldilocks.

Then she tried the little bed with the rabbits on it.

"Aaah, just right," she said. It was so comfortable that she immediately fell fast asleep.

Very soon The Three Bears returned home from their walk and were surprised to find the door open. They looked inside and noticed the bowls of porridge on the table.

"Somebody has been eating my porridge!" said Father Bear in a great, gruff, growling voice.

"Somebody has been eating my porridge!" said Mother Bear in a sweet, middle–sized voice.

"Somebody has been eating my porridge, and has eaten it all up!" cried Baby Bear in a squeaky, little voice.

Then they noticed the chairs had been moved.

"Somebody has been sitting in my chair!" said Father Bear in a great, gruff, growling voice.

"Somebody has been sitting in my chair!" said Mother Bear in a sweet, middle-sized voice.

"Somebody has been sitting in my chair, and has broken it all to bits!" sobbed Baby Bear in a squeaky, little voice, dripping tears on to the floor.

The Three Bears then heard the sound of snoring coming from upstairs. They tiptoed up the stairs and into the bedroom. They looked at the rumpled beds.

"Somebody has been lying on my bed!" said Father Bear in a great, gruff, growling voice.

"Somebody has been lying on my bed!" said Mother Bear in a sweet, middle-sized voice.

"Somebody has been lying on my bed, and she's still there!" wailed Baby Bear in a squeaky, little voice.

This commotion woke Goldilocks up with a start. Seeing The Three Bears she screamed,

"EEEEAAAWWAAAGHH!"

Goldilocks leaped out of bed and dived out of the nearest window. She landed in a blackberry bush, picked herself up, and ran home as fast as her legs would go.

The Three Bears lived happily ever after but they always locked their door when they went out, just in case.

LITTLE RED RIDING HOOD

Once upon a time there was a little girl who was called Little Red Riding Hood because she always wore a red cloak that her Grandma had made for her.

One day Little Red Riding Hood's mother said, "Your Grandma isn't very well. Why don't you go to her house and take her some cakes. You'd really cheer her up with a visit."

So Little Red Riding Hood packed a basket with cakes to take to her Grandma. As she waved goodbye, her mother warned her to be careful.

"Go straight through the woods to Grandma's House," said her mother. "Make sure you stay on the path and don't talk to any strangers."

Little Red Riding Hood agreed to do just as she was told but she hadn't gone far into the woods when she heard a rustling in the trees. A deep voice called, "Little girl, little girl, can you spare a minute?"

Little Red Riding Hood looked behind the trees and saw a large, smiling wolf. She remembered what her mother had said but the wolf really did look friendly.

"Where are you going on this lovely day, little girl?" asked the wolf.

"I'm going to my Grandma's house," said Little Red Riding Hood. "She's not very well and I'm taking her some cakes."

"How very kind of you," said the wolf. "Your Grandma will be so pleased." The wolf was very hungry and very clever and he had a wicked plan to eat both Little Red Riding Hood and her Grandma. With a big smile, he asked, "And where does your poor, old Grandma live?"

"She lives deep in the woods, at the very end of the path," replied Little Red Riding Hood.

"Why don't you pick a pretty bunch of flowers to take to your Grandma as well," said the wolf.

"What a good idea!" cried Little Red Riding Hood, and she ran here and there, gathering flowers together for her Grandma.

When Little Red Riding Hood was not looking, the wolf crept quietly away. Then he took a short cut through the trees to Grandma's house and quickly knocked on her door.

"Let me in, Grandma," squeaked the wolf in his highest voice. "I've brought some presents to cheer you up."

Grandma was delighted to hear Little Red Riding Hood's voice and, smiling happily, she opened the door. With a growl and a pounce, the wolf gobbled Grandma up in one big gulp.

"Mmm, yum, yum," he said. Then he hurried to Grandma's bedroom and searched her drawers until he found a big, pink nightgown and a frilly nightcap.

Quickly the wolf dressed himself in Grandma's clothes and leapt into bed just as he heard Little Red Riding Hood approaching the house. Little Red Riding Hood knocked on the door and when there was no answer, she called, "Grandma, where are you?"

"I'm in bed, my dear," called the wolf in his best 'old lady' voice. "Come right in, the door's not locked."

Little Red Riding Hood quickly lifted the latch and ran into her Grandma's bedroom. The curtains were pulled and the room was dark and gloomy.

"Grandma, are you all right?" asked Little Red Riding Hood.

"Of course, my dear," said the wolf, pulling the bed covers up to his chin. "I'm just resting."

As Little Red Riding Hood came closer to show the beautiful bunch of flowers she had picked, she noticed Grandma's ears.

"Grandma, what big ears you have!" she said.

"All the better to hear you with, my dear," said the wolf.

Then Little Red Riding Hood noticed Grandma's gleaming, yellow eyes.

"Grandma, what big eyes you have!"

"All the better to see you with, my dear," said the wolf.

"And Grandma, what big teeth you have!" cried Little Red Riding Hood.

"ALL THE BETTER TO EAT YOU WITH, MY DEAR!" growled the wolf as he leapt out of bed and gobbled up Little Red Riding Hood whole with a great big gulp.

With his belly full and fat, the wolf was soon fast asleep in Grandma's bed. A passing woodcutter was puzzled when he heard the wolf's loud snoring.

"That doesn't sound like the old lady," he thought. He stepped into Grandma's cottage and soon found the sleeping wolf. With a quick snip, he cut open the wolf's belly and out popped Little Red Riding Hood and Grandma, safe and sound. They were very grateful to the woodcutter and gave him the cakes to take home to his family. When Little Red Riding Hood went home she ran all the way and kept to the path, and she never talked to strangers again.

JACK AND THE BEANSTALK

There once lived a widow and her son, Jack, who were so poor they often had nothing to eat. Jack was a lazy boy and didn't care to work, so their fortunes went from bad to worse. One day they had nothing left to eat at all and so the poor widow reluctantly sent Jack to market to sell their cow.

"It's all we have left," she cried, "so make sure you get a good price for her."

As Jack walked along the road, he met a strange little man, dressed all in green.

"Is that cow for sale?" asked the little man.

"Yes," replied Jack, "I'm taking her to the market as we have no food to eat. Will you give me a good price?"

"It's a long walk to market," said the man. "I'll give you a bag of magic beans."

Very soon, lazy Jack was back home again with only a bag of beans to show his mother.

"Beans!" shouted his mother, and she threw them out of the window and sent Jack straight to bed.

The next morning Jack looked out of the window and saw an extraordinary sight; where his mother had thrown the beans, a huge beanstalk had grown, reaching far up into the sky. Quickly Jack ran outside and climbed higher and higher up the beanstalk. At the top, Jack found himself in a strange land and nearby stood an enormous castle.

"Perhaps I will be able to get something to eat here," thought hungry Jack, as he knocked on the great door.

The door was opened by a very tall woman.

"What do you want?" she said in a huge, gruff voice.

"Please, could you give me something to eat," said Jack.

"Well, you'll have to be quick," answered the woman. "If my husband sees you, he will have you for breakfast."

Just as Jack began to eat, there was the thump of heavy footsteps and the whole castle shook.

"Hide in here," said the woman, pushing Jack into the oven. As the giant came in, he roared:

"Fee, Fi, Fo, Fum,
I smell the blood of an Englishman.
Be he alive or be he dead,
I'll grind his bones to make my bread!"

"It's just the smell of your breakfast!" said his wife, handing him a huge plate of bacon and eggs. When the giant had finished eating, he called for his bags of gold. But no sooner had he started to count the coins than his eyes drooped and he began to snore. Jack jumped out of the oven, picked up a bag of gold and scrambled down the beanstalk.

Jack and his mother lived well but after a while all the gold was gone; so Jack climbed the beanstalk again and everything happened just as before. This time when the giant had finished eating, he called for his magic hen.

"Lay, little hen, lay," he ordered, and as Jack peeped out of the oven, he was amazed to see the hen lay a golden egg. Again, the giant soon fell asleep, so Jack seized his chance and stole the hen before climbing down the beanstalk.

Jack and his mother had everything they needed now, but one day Jack decided to climb the beanstalk and visit the giant's castle one last time. The minute the giant entered the castle, he sniffed the air and roared at the top of his voice:

"Fee, Fi, Fo, Fum,
I smell the blood of an Englishman.
Be he alive or be he dead,
I'll grind his bones to make my bread."

"No, no," called his wife. "There's no boy here. Let me fetch your magic harp, the music will soothe you."

As the harp played its own beautiful music, the giant fell fast asleep. Just as before, Jack nipped out of his hiding place and grabbed the harp. But as Jack ran from the castle, the harp squealed, "Master, master," and the giant woke up with a start. Roaring with rage, he chased after Jack. As Jack reached the bottom of the beanstalk, it started to shake violently. The giant was coming down after him!

"Mother, bring me the axe," Jack called. With a few mighty chops, he cut through the beanstalk. Down, down, down came the beanstalk and down came the giant too. And as the giant hit the earth, the ground split wide open and in he fell, never to be seen again. As for Jack and his mother, they were rich and happy for the rest of their lives.

INDEX

Titles are in *italics*. Where the title and the first line are the same, the first line only is listed.

ACKNOWLEDGEMENTS

The publishers would like to thank the copyright holders for permission to reproduce the following copyright material. Every effort has been made to trace the ownership of all copyrighted material and to secure the necessary permission to reprint these selections. In the event of any question arising as to the use of any material, the editor and publisher, while expressing regret for any inadvertent error, will be happy to make the necessary correction in future printings.

• Marie Louise Allen: 'The Mitten Song' from *A Pocket Full of Poems*, copyright © Marie Allen Howarth 1957. Reprinted by permission of HarperCollins*College Publishers* • Eleanor Farjeon: 'Good Night' from *Silver, Sand and Snow* (Michael Joseph) by permission of David Higham Associates • James Kirkup: 'Baby's Drinking Song' from The Listener, 1962 and *White Shadows, Black Shadows* (J M Dent and Sons, 1970) • Arnold Lobel: 'Little Pictures' from *Whiskers and Rhymes*, copyright © 1985 Arnold Lobel. Permission granted by the publisher Walker Books Ltd and Greenwillow Books, a division of William Morrow & Co, Inc.. • A A Milne: 'Happiness' from *When We Were Very Young* by A A Milne, published by Methuen Children's Books, © 1924 by E P Dutton, renewed by A A Milne 1952 • Joan Poulson: 'Patchy Bear' by permission of the author • Charles Thomson: 'Up to the Ceiling' from *Mr Mop Has a Floppy Top* (Stanford Book) reprinted by permission of the author.

First published in Great Britain
by HarperCollins Publishers Ltd in 1996
Compilation copyright © HarperCollins Publishers Ltd 1996

This edition published by Barnes & Noble, Inc.,
by arrangement with HarperCollins Publishers Ltd

1997 Barnes and Noble Books

M 10 9 8 7 6 5 4 3 2
ISBN: 0-7607-0632-8